THIS

SWEET PICKLES ™

BOOK BELONGS TO

HiLDeeTh

In the world of *Sweet Pickles,* each animal gets into a pickle because of an all too human personality trait.

This book is about Questioning Quail who can't make up her mind.

Other Books in the Sweet Pickles Series

Library of Congress Cataloging in Publication Data

Reinach, Jacquelyn.
  Quail can't decide.

  (Sweet Pickles series)
  SUMMARY: Quail can't make up her mind how to
spend her dollar.
  [1. Quails—Fiction] I. Title. II. Series.
PZ7.R2747Qai   [E]   77-7249
ISBN 0-03-021451-3

Printed in the United States of America

Weekly Reader Books' Edition

Weekly Reader Books presents

QUAIL
CAN'T
DECIDE

Written by Jacquelyn Reinach
Illustrated by Richard Hefter
Edited by Ruth Lerner Perle

Holt, Rinehart and Winston · New York

Quail had a dollar to spend and couldn't make up her mind how to spend it. She walked around in little circles, trying to decide what to do.

"I saw a big yellow plastic bracelet," she groaned. "And I love it!"

"But I need a new sugar bowl."

"But if I buy a new sugar bowl, then I can't buy a big yellow plastic bracelet."

"Or, maybe what I *really* want is a red scarf!"

"But I'm not sure!"

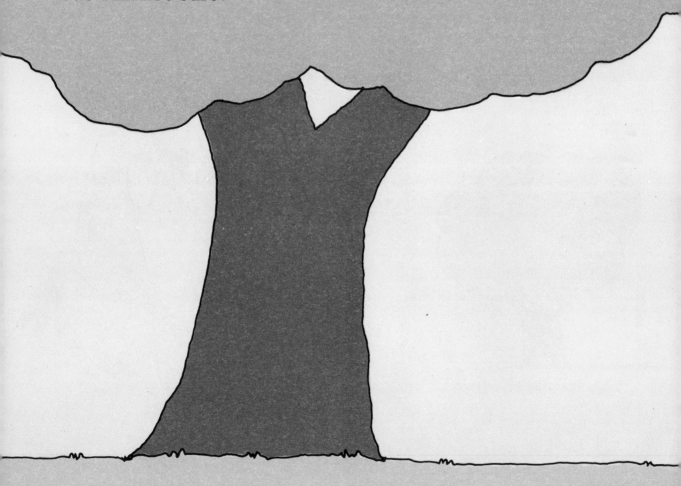

"You there! Quail!" called Xerus from the window next door. "Stop it! You're walking on my grass! Can't you read the signs? It's NOT ALLOWED!"

"Really?" said Quail. "I didn't notice.
I can't make up my mind what to buy with this dollar."

"You can *never* make up your mind!" yelled Xerus.
"Buy something you NEED! That's what you *should*
do with money."

"But how do I know?" asked Quail. "I *want* a big
yellow plastic bracelet. Does that mean I *need* one?
And I *need* a new sugar bowl, but I don't really
think I *want* one! And a red scarf would be nice, too."

Just then, Zebra zipped by. "Having fun?" he called.
"I don't think so," sighed Quail. "It's hard. I'm
trying to make a very important decision."

"What exactly are you trying to decide?" asked Zebra.
"I'm trying to decide how to spend this dollar,"
answered Quail. "Should I buy something I really
WANT or something I really NEED? I want a big
bracelet, but I need a new sugar bowl!"

"Well, what are you keeping your sugar in now?"
asked Zebra.

"A cup," said Quail.

"Well then, you *don't* need a new sugar bowl. You
just want one. And that answers your question,"
chuckled Zebra.

Zebra threw a kiss and went off.

Then Quail went downtown to go shopping.

In the department store, Dog was working behind a counter. He looked at Quail and frowned. "I doubt that I can," said Dog, "but if I could, can I help you?"

"Oh, would you?" asked Quail. "Would you tell me what I can buy for this dollar?"

"Not much," said Dog, shaking his head. "Except for this special sale here."

"Oh!" said Quail. "That's exactly what I'm looking for!" She tried on a big yellow plastic bracelet.

Then she took it off and examined a blue sugar bowl.

Then she put back the sugar bowl and tried on the bracelet again.

Then she walked over to the door to see the bracelet in a better light. Lion was coming in.

"Oh, Lion!" said Quail. "Should I buy this yellow bracelet?"

"Of course!" smiled Lion. "If that's what would make you happy, buy it!"

"Or," continued Quail, "should I get a new sugar bowl?"

"Certainly," said Lion. "If that's what you want, get it!"
"But I just don't know which to buy!" said Quail.

"Tough luck!" cried Nightingale. "Hey, why don't you buy a red scarf like mine?"

"I was thinking of that, too," said Quail.

"Tough luck," chortled Nightingale. "I just bought the last one! And you can't have it. Nyaaa!"

"Well, how long would it take to order another scarf?" asked Quail.

"About a week," said Dog. "Would you like me to order a red scarf? I might be able to do that."

Quail sighed and walked around in a little circle. "I don't know," she said. "I'm just not sure. I think I have my heart set on the big yellow plastic bracelet."

"Fine!" said Dog. "Will you take it, or shall I send it?"
"Don't rush me!" cried Quail. "I haven't made up my mind yet!"

Alligator pounded on the counter. "This is ridiculous," she screamed. "Nobody else can get waited on and it's your fault, Quail!"

"I'm sorry," said Quail. "It's so hard deciding what to do with this dollar!"

"Why, that shouldn't be hard at all," said Rabbit. "A dollar is really not very much money. But, if you put that dollar into a savings account, it will earn interest. Rabbit took out his calculator and pressed the buttons. "Why, in ten years," said Rabbit, "you could have a dollar *ninety-seven*! That's almost double your money!"

"And double my problems!" said Quail. "*Then* what would I buy?"

"Spending money is certainly a big worry," agreed Walrus.

Quail burst into tears, rushed out of the store and ran across the street into the park.
Everybody followed her.

"It's wonderful to have a good cry!" said Moose.
"You'll feel so much better!"

"Why cry?" said Kangaroo. "I know how you can feel better right away!"

"How?" asked Quail tearfully.

"Give me the dollar!" he grinned. "Then your worries will be over! Haw, haw!"

Quail sobbed harder.

"There, there," comforted Elephant. "Maybe what you really want is raisins. Trunks full of raisins."

"Or buy a lottery ticket," smiled Pig. "I'm positive today's a lucky day!"

"But if I buy a lottery ticket, I can't buy raisins," sniffed Quail. "And if I buy raisins, I won't have a big yellow plastic bracelet, which is what I really would like if I could only make up my mind!"

"Listen!" shouted Octopus. "This is outrageous, letting everybody tell you what to do. It's *your* money, Quail, and you obviously want a bracelet. Go and get it!"

Quail smiled. She jumped up and went back to the department store. "I'll take the bracelet!" she cried.

"I'll take the dollar," said Dog.

"Oh, dear, I hope I'm doing the right thing," sighed Quail.

"Remember," warned Dog, "all sales are final. No refunds."

Quail gave Dog the dollar and took the bracelet.

But as Quail was leaving the store, she had a funny feeling in her stomach. "Oh, dear," she thought. "Maybe the bracelet won't look right with my other jacket. Maybe it's too big. Maybe it's too yellow. Maybe I was wrong to get it!"

She bumped into Vulture.

"Wow! That bracelet is gorgeous!" cried Vulture.

"You like it?" asked Quail.

"I love it!" cried Vulture.

"Then take it. It's yours for a dollar!" said Quail.
She quickly handed the bracelet to Vulture. "Anyway,
it will look better on you," she said.

"That's true," grinned Vulture. He gave Quail a
dollar and went off admiring himself and the big
yellow plastic bracelet.

"WELL!" said Quail. "Well!" she said again. "I *finally* made up my mind about the bracelet!"
"NOW, I only have to decide how to spend this dollar!"

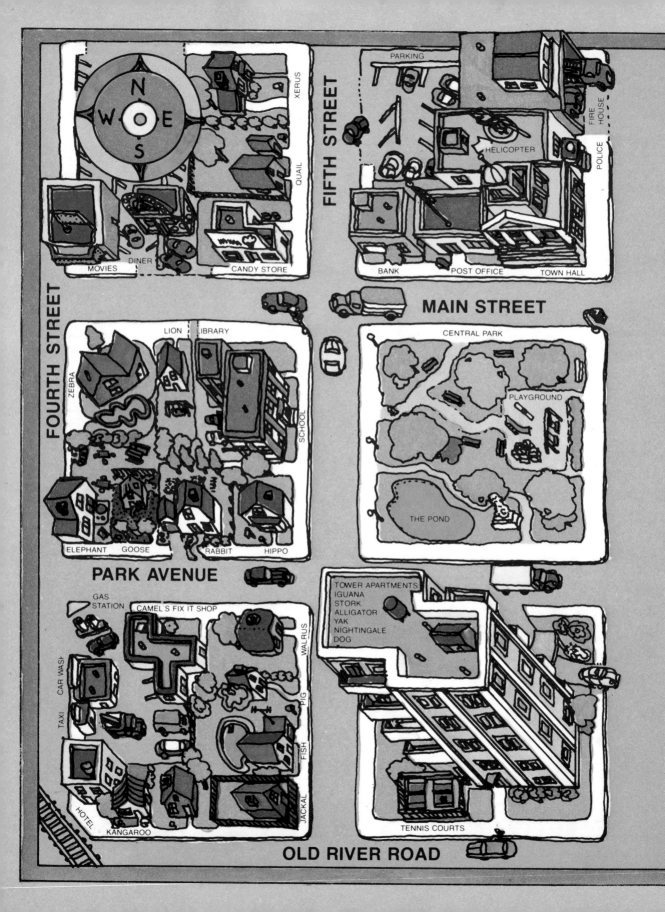